My Window is Open

"A Short Inspirational Bedtime Story"

Written by: Sean Curry

My
Window
is Open

My window is open, allowing

sunlight to come in,

To hear sweet sounds of birds singing, while raindrops touch my skin.

My window is open, to see a rainbow after a storm,

To receive a nice cool
breeze on summer nights
when the sky is warm.

My window is open to
see funny-shaped
clouds go drifting by.

To see the sun begin to
set bringing forth
a star-filled sky.

My window is open, allowing
me to see great
lights and much more.

So open your window, then take a good look, and when you fall asleep, your dreams will soar.

I can be anything.

Print information available on the last page

Rev. date: 04/09/2019

To order additional copies of this book, contact:
Xlibris
1-888-795-4274
www.Xlibris.com
Orders@Xlibris.com

Printed in the United States
By Bookmasters